KING ARTHUR

by

JEREMY SMITH

Gododdin

Historia Brittonum

ARTHUR - MAN & MYTH

The legend of King Arthur is a bewitching blend of history and myth. The story we know today has been added to by generations of storytellers. It tells of a king who drew a sword from a stone to claim power, vanquished all on the battlefield and held court in Camelot, before eventually being betrayed by his knight Lancelot and Queen Guinevere. There is little evidence to back up this story, but a few early texts speak of a great warrior king that existed between 400-600 AD. This figure may have been the real king behind the myth of Arthur.

King Arthur

THE FIRST MENTION OF ARTHUR

The *Gododdin* was written by the British poet Aneirin around 600 AD. In it, he praises a courageous man who died battling the Angles, but says that "he was no Arthur." Aneirin is making a comparison between this soldier and a great warrior called Arthur. Another piece of writing that speaks of a warrior who might be the legendary king is the *Historia Brittonum.* Written around 830 AD by a monk from North Wales called Nennius, it states that "Arthur was leader of battles."

WORDS FROM THE CHURCH

In the 6th Century AD, a monk called Gildas wrote a stinging attack on British society called *De Excidio Britanniae (On the Ruin and Conquest of Britain).* In it, Gildas mentions the Battle of Badon, a battle that appears in most Arthurian stories. Some historians even think that the monk names King Arthur. He writes about "the bear's stronghold," and in Welsh, the word Arth means bear.

Glastonbury Abbey, home to the monk Gildas

ANNALES CAMBRIAE

These Welsh annuals (a type of yearbook) were written around the 10th century. They make two references to a warrior called Arthur. The first tells us that Arthur was victorious at the Battle of Badon, while the second says that Arthur and Medraud perished during the Battle of Camlann.

The Annales Cambriae

GEOFFREY OF MONMOUTH

In the 12th century AD, the teacher Geoffrey of Monmouth wrote a famous work about King Arthur called the *Historia Regum Britanniae*. In this story, Arthur not only defeats the Saxons, but raises a lavish court, wields a magical sword and is mortally wounded by his nephew Mordred, before being carried to the mystical Isle of Avalon (*see page 27*). Geoffrey of Monmouth is also chiefly responsible for the invention of Merlin in a poem called *Vita Merlini* (1150).

An illustration of Geoffrey of Monmouth

THE GREAT ROMANCERS

By the end of the 12th century, European writers such as Chrétien de Troyes had added new elements into the Arthur story, such as the quest for the Holy Grail (*see p22-23*), and the court of Camelot (*see p8-9*). But it was Sir Thomas Malory who was responsible for the modern story of King Arthur. In *Le Morte D'Arthur*, written in 1470 and published in 1485, gives us an Arthurian story filled with passion, honour and betrayal. To appeal to the audience of the time, Malory conjured up romantic images of clashing broadswords and fields of knights dressed in gleaming armour. Thanks to the invention of the first printing press by William Caxton in 1477, the book was widely distributed and became extremely popular.

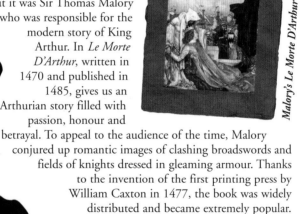

Malory's Le Morte D'Arthur

THE VICTORIANS & ARTHUR

In the 19th Century, the Victorians fell in love again with the story of Arthur. Tales of knightly chivalry and magic were painted during the Pre-Raphaelite art movement, while romantic writers such as Tennyson wrote about the great king in his book *Idylls of the King*.

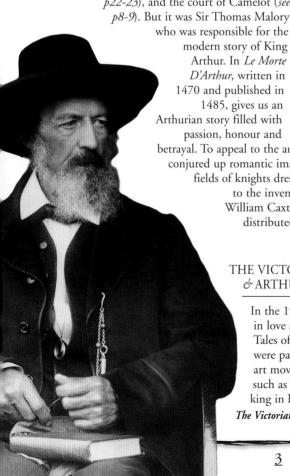

The Victorian poet Tennyson

TIMELINE

AD 43
Romans invade Britain

AD 122
Work on Hadrian's Wall begins

AD 360
Britain faces attacks from Picts and Scots

AD 401
Roman troops withdrawn from Britain

AD 449
Saxons invade

AD 486
Battle of Mount Badon and birth of Gildas

AD 529
Gildas' De Excidio Britanniae is published

AD 539
Battle of Camlann takes place, according to Annales Cambriae

AD 600
Aneirin composes Goddodin

1136-38
Geoffrey of Monmouth's Historia Regum Britanniae written

1150
Geoffrey of Monmouth's Vita Merlini written

1155
Wace writes Roman de Brut

1170-91
Chrétien de Troyes writes five Arthurian romances

1215-35
Vulgate Cycle written

14XX
Poem of Sir Gawain and the Green Knight written

1485
Thomas Malory's Le Morte D'Arthur is published

1859
Tennyson's Idylls of The King published

1958
T.H. White's The Once and Future King published.

INVASION OF THE PICTS

At the same time that the Scots were invading from Ireland, England was under attack from the Picts from Scotland. These land-hungry people made a series of raids over a barrier called Hadrian's Wall (built in the 2nd century AD by the Roman emperor Hadrian to keep invaders from the North out of England) to claim land in Northern England. The presence of ruined Roman signal stations along the north-east coast of England shows just how dangerous the Picts were considered to be.

Hadrian's Wall

ARRIVAL OF THE SAXONS

Under constant assault from marauding invaders from Ireland and Scotland, the authorities invited over Germanic mercenaries to defend their kingdom. Composed of three tribes – Angles, Saxons and Jutes – they plundered through the South East of England, eventually forcing the Romans to abandon the country. Writers like Gildas hint at their brutality, saying their name is one "not to be spoken, hated by man and God."

A map showing the flow of invaders into Brit.

LIFE FOR THE POOR

Life during the 5th century AD for the poor in Britain after the Romans had left was a difficult time. Gildas speaks of five tyrant kings, unjust rulers who exploited their subjects. He gives them nicknames such as "the red butcher" and "dragon of the island." Some of these rulers even took slaves from the poor for human sacrifices to serve as an example to the rest of the population.

A Roman coin showing child sacrifice

LIFE FOR THE RICH

The wealthy in post-Roman Britain enjoyed an enviable lifestyle. Archaeologists have found traces of wild honey, bread, pig's meat and oysters dating from around the 5th century AD. Bottles dug up suggest that in addition they guzzled huge quantities of vintage wine. Gildas also tells us that the elite drove horse-drawn carriages, and "regarded themselves as superior to the rest of man."

A Roman mosaic showing lifestyles of the rich

BRITAIN AT THE TIME OF ARTHUR

ritain at the time when many people believe Arthur may have lived was a country in crisis. A peaceful period of Roman settlement which had lasted over 300 years was coming to a violent and bloody end. Arguments were settled with the sword and uprisings brutally crushed. In the middle of the 5th century, England was being attacked by the Picts and Scots. The Roman authorities invited three tribes of mercenaries over from Germany to help them restore order, but with disastrous effects. These visitors turned on their hosts, and rampaged through Southern England. Eventually the Romans were driven out of England, and replaced by a system whereby each region was ruled by a different king. These kings had no proper authority, and were usually just popular and powerful men who had taken advantage of the political chaos to set themselves up as local rulers.

ROMAN BRITAIN

Around AD 43, the Romans arrived on English shores to conquer and colonize. This advanced civilisation built baths, forts, temples and other great monuments, and imposed a civilized way of life on the natives. Education spread through towns and cities, and Latin was introduced as the first language. But then, in AD 410, the Emperor Claudius withdrew his men from Britain because of constant attack from the Picts and Scots, leaving the island dangerously exposed to invaders.

Roman ruins at Vindolanda in Northumberland

INVASION OF THE SCOTS

The label Scots is rather confusingly given to a race of people from Ireland who began raiding Britain between 300-500 AD. The name may come from an Irish verb meaning "to raid." These Scots settled in numbers in Argyll, Scotland.

Argyll in Scotland

CHRISTIANITY

By the 5th century AD, the Christian religion brought over by the Romans had become established in Britain. Churches and villas with Christian motifs appeared everywhere, and monasteries also sprung up. In his Historia Brittonum, the monk Nennius writes about a Christian warrior called Arthur, telling us "he carried the image of St Mary on his shoulders, and the pagans were turned to flight."

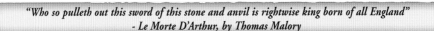

THE RISE OF ARTHUR

With power in post-Roman Britain divided between several kings, the country was extremely unstable. Arthurian stories say that a young man called Arthur came forward to claim the crown, ushering in a period of more than half a century of peace.

THE SWORD IN THE STONE

According to Geoffrey of Monmouth, to determine the true king of Britain, the wizard Merlin (*see pages 10-11*) erected a stone with a sword in it, and invited anybody to try to remove the weapon. All the kings tried but noone could shift the sword. Then a young man called Arthur passed by. He was working as a squire for a knight called Kay, and was travelling to meet his master at a joust. Arthur had forgotten to bring Kay's special sword with him, and was worrying about how to explain this to his master. When he noticed the sword sticking out from the stone, Arthur rushed over, and immediately drew it from its block. Arriving at the joust, he pulled out the sword to give it to Kay, but it was instantly recognised, and the young Arthur was proclaimed the true king of Britain.

A Victorian recreation of the Sword in the Stone

EXCALIBUR

When Arthur smashed his sword in combat some years later, Merlin took him to a mysterious lake where a Lady of the Lake emerged from the water. In her hand she clasped a dazzling sword called Excalibur, and a gold scabbard. The scabbard was considered just as precious as Excalibur, because Merlin had told Arthur that anyone wearing it would never shed blood on the battlefield.

LIST OF BATTLES

King Arthur had twelve battles against the Saxons:

1. *Mouth of the River Glein*

2-5. *The River Douglas in Linnuis*

6. *River Bassas*

7. *Cat Coity Celidon*

8. *Guinnion*

9. *City of the Legions*

10. *River Tribruit*

11. *Mount Agned*

12. *Battle of Badon*

BATTLE OF BADON

Arthur's most famous battle was the Battle of Badon. It took place towards the end of the 5th Century AD, and was a final battle against the Saxons. Gildas tells us that after Badon "war with the Anglo-Saxons had ceased." By the time the battle was fought, Arthur had already developed a reputation as a fearless leader, famous for both his military prowess and his Christian goodness.

Illustration of the Battle of Badon by George Wooliscroft Rhead and Louis Rhead

The Taking of Excalibur by John Duncan

BATTLE OF BEDEGRAINE

After Arthur crushed the Saxons, he faced immediate danger from several directions. Britain was still a deeply divided place, with many ambitious rivals wanting to replace Arthur as king. In *Le Morte D'Arthur*, Malory tells us that one of Arthur's key battles was in a forest called Bedegraine. There, Arthur and his soldiers faced an uprising by 11 British kings. Armed with thousands of troops, they laid siege to a castle belonging to a supporter of Arthur. But, helped by Merlin, Arthur's men drove his enemies out of the forest, inflicting dreadful wounds on them.

Nigel Terry ready for battle as King Arthur in the film Excalibur *(1981)*

CAMELOT

Camelot lay at the heart of Arthur's kingdom. It was a splendid city with an almost impregnable castle built on a scale that had never been seen before. It was here that Arthur held court, and here where his knights were called to the Round Table (*see pages 12-13*). Lavish banquets were held, jousts between the greatest knights took place and government was carried out. Although historians cannot agree on the site of Arthur's capital, the name Camelot endures today as a symbol of goodness, virtue and ideal government all over the world.

CAMELOT THE CAPITAL

After being crowned King, Arthur chose Camelot as the seat of his new government. Camelot was also a base from which his knights rode out, seeking adventure. They would return to regale the Court with exciting tales of valour and conquest.

CAMELOT IN WRITING

The two great Arthurian writers both suggest different locations for Arthur's capital. Malory places Camelot in Winchester, possibly because a Round Table hangs in the castle there. Geoffrey suggests that an unnamed capital lies at Tintagel. Unfortunately, historians are sceptical about both claims, as there is no evidence of a castle at Tintagel before 1300, and the Round Table in Winchester dates from around the same time.

DATING THE EVIDENCE

Archaeologists use several methods to date ancient sites and artefacts. Dendrochronology is the technique of dating by counting tree rings. Each ring represents a year's growth, so the rings can be counted to reveal just how old a tree is. Timber used in houses can be counted to find out how old the building is. Another technique is neutron activation analysis. By bombarding an object with gamma rays, archaeologists can find out not only when an artefact was made, but where it was made. Finally, archeologists use carbon dating to date living things, such as wood and bone. Because carbon decays at a certain rate, archaeologists can find out how old something is by measuring the amount of carbon left in it.

CHRÉTIEN DE TROYES

Until the late 12th century, no mention had been made of a place called Camelot in any surviving manuscripts. Then the French poet Chrétien de Troyes introduced the idea of a noble court of that name in five Arthurian romances written between 1260 and 1280.

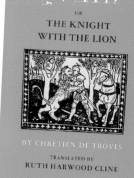

A romance by Chretien de Troyes

A dig at Cadbury Hill

CADBURY HILL AS CAMELOT?

Cadbury Hill is an Iron Age hill fort in Somerset. In 1542 Henry VIII's aide John Leland wrote that local people believed that Cadbury had been the site of Camelot. An archaeological dig in the 1960s confirmed that the camp was in use around 500 AD but there is little to connect Cadbury Hill specifically to Arthur. It is possible that the link between Cadbury Hill and Camelot comes from the names of two villages near the site – Queen Camel and West Camel.

The remains of the bath house at Viroconium

Arthur's castle at Camelot from the 1967 film Camelot.

A WELSH CAMELOT

The ruins of Viroconium in Wales are all that remain of a Roman city built there around AD 150. But a dig in the 1960s uncovered a number of post-Roman, two-storey buildings, telling us that the city was completely rebuilt around AD 420, close to the age of Arthur. Viroconium's site, on the banks of the River Severn, mean that it would have place of great strategic importance during Roman times, and could possibly have been the site of Camelot.

MERLIN

Nicol Williamson as Merlin in the film Excalibur *(1981)*

MERLIN THE MAGICIAN

According to Geoffrey of Monmouth, Merlin's mother was a princess, but his father was an incubus, an evil spirit who cast a spell on the princess so he could seduce her while she slept. Other stories suggest that Merlin was the result of a pact between a group of devils to create a half-demon child. Their plan is ruined, however, when a priest steps in to bless Merlin's mother. Merlin is born with supernatural powers, but he remains good, rather than evil.

The wizard Merlin was King Arthur's magician, counsellor and closest friend. Geoffrey of Monmouth places him at the centre of Arthur's story, making him responsible for the sword in the stone contest and foretelling the downfall of Arthur's kingdom. Some historians think that the character of Merlin was actually based on a Welsh bard called Myddrin. Mentioned in later Welsh literature, Myddrin may have existed around 400-600 AD, the time of Arthur. Bards were a type of poet who were highly regarded at the time, and were thought to have magical powers.

VORTIGERN'S TOWER

After the Romans left Britain, a king called Vortigern came to the throne. In his *Historia Regum Britanniae,* Geoffrey of Monmouth tells us that Vortigern planned to build a great tower, but every time it was finished, it immediately collapsed. His counsellors advised him that a sacrifice of a fatherless child was needed to break this curse. Merlin was chosen, but he told the king that the reason the tower kept falling was that two dragons slept in a pool beneath the ground. When the ground was dug up, two fighting dragons emerged and flew away. From this moment, the child Merlin began making prophecies, including the eventual downfall of King Vortigern.

A 15th-century illustration showing the two dragons escaping from Vortigern's tower

STONEHENGE

Geoffrey of Monmouth tells us that eventually King Vortigern was defeated, just as Merlin had prophesized. To mark this occasion, the wizard told the new king Aurelius he must bring over a set of stones called the Giant's Dance from Ireland, and make a monument from them. The result was Stonehenge. Today we know that this story cannot be true, because the stones have been scientifically dated back thousands of years.

MERLIN & ARTHUR

After the death of Aurelius, Monmouth says that the new king Uther Pendragon asks for Merlin's assistance to help him seduce a married woman called Igraine. Merlin casts a spell that transforms Uther into Igraine's husband, and Igraine gives birth to Uther's child, Arthur. Merlin takes the baby and gives him to Sir Ector – father of Kay (*see page 6*)– to bring up. It is Merlin who is also responsible for Arthur's crowning as king, setting up the sword in the stone contest (*see page 6*). In Geoffery of Monmouth's writings, the wizard also accompanies the King to Avalon after the Battle of Camlann (*see page 28*).

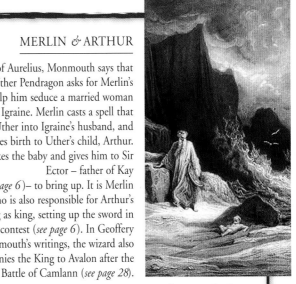

An illustration by Gustav Doré showing Merlin finding Arthur

MERLIN & NIMUE

There are several different accounts of the downfall of Merlin. In one, Merlin becomes infatuated with a young girl called Nimue (Vivian), whom he takes on as an apprentice. Merlin teaches her his most powerful spells, but Nimue betrays the wizard and uses the spells to trap him in an enchanted sleep.

The Beguiling of Merlin by Edward Burne-Jones

MERLIN'S GRAVE & GHOST

Many sites claim to be the last resting place of Merlin. In England they include the grounds of Marlborough College and Tintagel Castle, while in Brittany, three tombs claim to hold his bones. In Wales the bleak and remote Isle of Bardsey is a candidate, while some people say Merlin's Hill Cave in Carmarthen is still haunted by the wizard's ghost. Another story says that Merlin's treasure lies in a cave in Snowdonia. It is said that it will be discovered by "a young man, blue of eye and fair of hair." When such a man finds the place, a bell will sound and the cave will open.

Rugged Snowdonia in North Wales

THE WILD MAN OF THE WOODS

Geoffrey of Monmouth tells a different story about Merlin's last days in a poem called Vita Merlini (1150). *In this tale, Merlin goes mad after the battle of Ardeydd in Scotland. Driven insane by what he sees on the battlefield, he flees to the woods to live as a hermit. Eventually his sanity returns, and his sister Ganieda builds him an observatory from which to gaze up at the stars.*

SEATING ARRANGEMENTS

The Round Table allowed Arthur's knights to sit in a circle. This meant that there were no arguments about who should be sitting where according to rank. Some historians suggest that the knights sat inside the table, with the king seated separately in the centre, as shown in this woodcut illustration.

An illustration of the Round Table taken from an 1816 edition of Malory's Le Morte D'Arthur

THE CODE OF CHIVALRY

The Arthurian stories of Chrétien and Malory helped to develop an ideal of knightly conduct called the Code of Chivalry. It demanded that knights should not simply be strong and brave on the battlefield, but be modest and generous to others, gentle and courteous to the ladies, and show powers of endurance. Above all the Code said that knights should show unwavering loyalty to the king. Jousting tournaments were held to give knights the perfect stage on which to prove their worth.

An anonymous illustration showing a knight ready to joust

THE ROUND TABLE TODAY

For hundreds of years, visitors to Winchester Castle come face to face with a round table in the Great Hall. It was redecorated by Henry VII's son, Henry VIII, in honour of his dead brother Arthur. Over time the table became regarded as the original Round Table of King Arthur. However, archaeological dating revealed that the table dates from the 13th century AD and not from the age of Arthur.

The Round Table in Winchester Castle

THE SIEGE PERILOUS

There was a special seat at the Round Table called the Siege Perilous. It was reserved for the knight who discoved the true meaning of the Holy Grail (see pages 24-25), and is eventually claimed by Galahad. In Le Morte D'Arthur, Malory tells us that the chair was made by Merlin.

THE ROUND TABLE & GUINEVERE

The Round Table was introduced into the story of King Arthur by the Jersey poet Wace in his book *Roman de Brut* (1155). A wedding gift from Guinevere's father, it became a symbol of Arthur's Camelot. According to some writers, it could seat over 1,600 knights. Many of the men who sat around this great table were invented by the French poet Chrétien de Troyes.

ARTHUR'S KNIGHTS

Several stories tell us that when he became king, Arthur instructed Merlin to find at least 50 knights to serve him. These knights included Kay, Bedivere, Lancelot, Tristan, Perceval, Griflet, Gawain, Aglovale, and Lucan. At the wedding feast of Arthur and Guinevere, they sat at a table with their names written in gold letters around it.

A 14th-century painting showing two knights offering their services to King Arthur

GUINEVERE - ARTHUR'S QUEEN

Arthur's queen is given the name Guinevere by Geoffrey of Monmouth. After Arthur's overwhelming victory at Badon, against Merlin's advice, he marries Guinevere, daughter of King Leodegrance of Cameliard. At the wedding, King Leodegrance presents Arthur with the Round Table as a gift.

The marriage of Arthur and Guinevere in the film Excalibur *(1981)*

LANCELOT

YOUNG LANCELOT

According to Thomas Malory, Lancelot is the son of the French king Ban of Benwick. When he is a baby, Lancelot is separated from his mother, and found by the magical Lady of the Lake, who raises him and gives him the title of Sir Lancelot of the Lake. Lancelot grows up to be a great warrior, slaying both dragons and human enemies.

Lancelot in battle in the film Excalibur (1981)

The dashing Lancelot is the most famous of Arthur's knights. His story is first mentioned in the 12th century by Chrétien de Troyes. He was regarded as the perfect example of chivalry and courtly virtue, and Arthur's most faithful servant. But Lancelot is equally well known for the betrayal of King Arthur through his affair with Queen Guinevere.

ELAINE OF ASTALOT

Lancelot is famous as a great lover, and breaks many hearts during his lifetime. One of these was the lady Elaine of Astalot. She meets the dashing knight on his way to a tournament, and begs him to marry her. When Lancelot declines, Elaine offers to become his mistress, but when he refuses again, she dies of grief and her body floats down the river to Camelot.

Elaine of Astalot was immortalised in John Waterhouse's painting **The Lady of Shalot**

ELAINE OF CORBENIC

According to Malory, Lancelot is tricked into an affair with King Pelles' daughter, Elaine of Corbenic. The king wants his daughter to produce a great son (*see p24*), and asks a witch to cast a spell that transforms Elaine for one night into Lancelot's love Guinevere. The couple spend the night together, and Elaine later gives birth to a son called Galahad.

Above: **Elaine of Corbenic** *by W. Russell Flint*

JOYOUS GARD

In *Le Morte D'Arthur*, Lancelot establishes a reputation as a bold and heroic knight when he single-handedly frees the castle Dolorous Gard from the clutches of an evil tyrant. There he finds a tomb with a slab bearing the inscription "This slab shall never be raised by the efforts of any man's hand but by him who shall conquer this Dolorous Castle, and the name of that man is written here beneath." When Lancelot slides back the stone, he reads the words "Here shall be Launcelot du Lac, the son of King Ban of Benwick." Lancelot renames the castle Joyous Gard, and makes it his home.

Bamburgh Castle in Northumberland, thought to be the real Joyous Gard

LANCELOT & GUINEVERE

Most stories tell us that the downfall of Lancelot begins when he becomes infatuated with Arthur's queen, Guinevere. After the queen is abducted by a knight called Meliagaunce, Lancelot rides to her rescue. However, the two fall deeply in love and a tempestuous affair begins. Chrétien tells us that "from the moment he caught sight of her, he did not turn or take his eyes and face from her."

A painting by W. Russell Flint, showing the rescue of Guinevere

FLIGHT FROM CAMELOT

When the two lovers are discovered, Lancelot flees Camelot, while the Queen is sentenced to burning at the stake. But as the flames start to crackle, the knight returns to snatch her from the fire. Lancelot and Guinevere escape to Joyous Gard, but the knight Gawain convinces Arthur to pursue the couple, and war breaks out between the two great knights (*see p16-17*).

The Accolade *by Edmund Blair Leighton*

THE FRENCH & LANCELOT
Unlike many of the characters in the story of Arthur, Lancelot is an almost exclusively French creation. He first appears in Chrétien de Troyes **Eric et Enide**, *and he is also the hero of Chrétien's* **Le Chevalier de la Charrete** (The Knight of the Cart). *Lancelot is the most popular of the knights among French writers, because of his chivalry.*

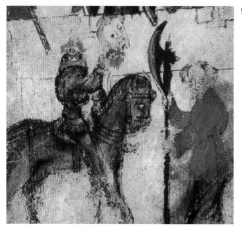

An early painting showing Gawain beheading the Green Knight

LANCELOT & GAWAIN

Lancelot and Gawain were great friends who became sworn enemies when Lancelot killed one of Gawain's brothers who discovered him in the arms of Guinevere. A fierce supporter of Arthur, Gawain follows the king to France when Arthur pursues Lancelot and Guinevere. Eventually the two knights meet in combat, and Lancelot fells Gawain with a blow to the head.

Part of a tapestry called **The Failure of Sir Gawaine** *by Edward Burne-Jones*

THE GREEN KNIGHT

Sir Gawain and the Green Knight was written by an anonymous English poet around 1400. This story illustrates the importance of knightly virtue, and tells of the appearance of a Green Knight at Arthur's New Year's feast at Camelot. The Green Knight invites Arthur's knights to trade blows with him. Gawain takes up the challenge and decapitates the Green Knight, who calmy walks over and picks up his head, telling Gawain to meet him on New Year's morning to face the Green Knight's sword. On the way to meet the Green Knight, Gawain lodges with a lord named Bertilak and his wife. Bertilak and Gawain agree to give to the other what they receive during the knight's stay. On the first day, Bertilak's wife gives Gawain a kiss, which Gawain passes on to her husband later that day. On the second day she kisses Gawain twice, and on the third day three times, also giving him some green lace which has protective powers. Each time Gawain passes on the kisses, but he keeps the green lace. When he meets the Green Knight, Gawain is struck three times by his sword. The first two blows miss his neck, while the third merely grazes it. The Green Knight reveals himself to be Bertilak, who tells Gawain that if Gawain had given up the green lace, all three blows would have missed him.

GAWAIN'S GHOST

The ghost of Gawain is said to wander at Spanish Head on the Isle of Man. It is even said that it bears the marks of the Green Knight's axe upon its neck.

Spanish Head on the Isle of Man

CELTIC GAWAIN
The tale of the Green knight and the Carle of Carlisle is probably based on ancient Celtic mythology. In one Irish tale, Cu Roi, the King of Munster, arrives in the form of a giant to challenge three of his champions to behead him, on the condition that he could do the same to them afterwards. The first two champions slice off his head, but refuse to let the giant slash his sword at them. Only Cuchullain keeps his side of the bargain. At this point, Cu Roi reveals who he really is and proclaims Cuchullain his one true champion.

GAWAIN

Gawain and the Loathly Lady by E.B. Bensell

Gawain is one of Arthur's most famous knights. In most French stories, his feats are overshadowed by Lancelot's, but many English authors made Gawain the hero of their stories. His mother Morgause (*see page 20*) is the King's sister, and as Arthur's nephew, Gawain is treated favourably at Camelot. Described as "one of the most faultless of fellows" in Malory's *Le Morte D'Arthur*, Gawain was a great warrior, whose strength it was believed increased greatly before noon, and ebbed away as the Sun set. Gawain was also once Lancelot's closest friend, but the two became bitter enemies.

THE LOATHLY LADY

The knight Gawain agrees to marry a lady called Ragnell to save Arthur from a perilous situation. But when he meets her, Gawain discovers she is hideous. When night falls, however, Ragnell turns from a hag into a beautiful lady. Ragnell tells Gawain that she can be beautiful by day, or by night, but that he must choose. Gawain declines, and generously allows her to choose. Because of this, Ragnell tells the knight that she will be beautiful all the time.

A Roman Spatha sword and scabbard, the weapon of choice during the age of Arthur

CARLE OF CARLISLE

The Carle of Carlisle is a 17th-century poem from a collection called the *Percy Folio Manuscript*. It tells the story of Gawain, Kay and Bishop Baldwin's stay at a giant's castle. The giant (the Carle) reveals to them that he has been made this size by magic, and that the only way to break the spell is to remove his head. Gawain draws his sword and decapitates the giant, and, as told, the Carle returns to his normal stature. As a reward, the Carle grants Gawain his beautiful daughter's hand in marriage.

LOVE POTIONS

The King of Ireland, Anguish, offers his daughter Iseult's hand in marriage to anyone who will rid his kingdom of a monstrous dragon. Tristan accepts the challenge, and claims Iseult's hand, not for himself, but for his Uncle Mark. But on the journey back to Cornwall, the couple drink a love potion meant for Iseult and King Mark, and fall deeply in love.

How Sir Tristram Drank of the Love Drink *by Aubrey Beardsley*

TRISTAN & ISEULT

The tale of Tristan and Iseult was one of the most popular love stories of the Middle Ages. In most accounts, Tristan is a knight of the Round Table, in service with his uncle Mark, King of Cornwall. Handsome, clever and talented at hunting, jousting and playing the harp, Tristan rushes to protect his uncle when he is challenged to a duel. But Tristan sustains terrible wounds, and retreats to Ireland, where he is nursed by the King of Ireland's beautiful daughter, the princess Iseult. It is this relationship that eventually brings him into deadly conflict with his uncle.

DOOMED LOVERS

Although Iseult marries Mark when she returns to England, she continues her affair with Tristan for many years. On many occasions their relationship is nearly uncovered, and eventually a heartbroken Tristan flees to Brittany, knowing Iseult will never leave Mark. There, he meets and weds a woman called Iseult of the White Hands, but their marriage is never consummated.

Tristan and Iseult *by John Waterhouse*

DEATH OF TRISTAN

When King Mark discovers Tristan's affair with his wife, he is furious. Mark pursues his treacherous nephew and mortally wounds him in a duel. While he is dying, Tristan calls for his first love, Mark's wife Iseult. The knight asks that if she comes to him, her ship should carry a white sail. Tristan's lover does as he says but the jealous Iseult of the White Hands deceives her husband, telling him instead that his sweetheart's ship bears only black sails. Tristan dies heartbroken. Some people think that Tristan's grave has been discovered. Near Castle Dore in Cornwall, there lies a stone which is said to bear his name. The Latin inscription reads "*Drustanus hic iacit cunomori filius*", which translates as "*Here lies Drustan, son of Cunomorus*".

The Death of Tristan *by F. Madox Brown*

A poster from a European production of Wagner's **Tristan and Isolde** *opera, and inset, a cover of his opera score*

WAGNER'S OPERA

The tragic story of Tristan and Iseult inspired many artists and musicains in the 19th century. In 1871 the German composer Richard Wagner wrote an opera telling their story, called *Tristan and Isolde.*

ADVENTURES OF TRISTAN

Tristan is a great knight who eventually becomes part of Arthur's Round Table. He fights many battles, including one in which he kills Sir Hemison, a knight of Morgan Le Fay. In other tales he confronts monstrous beasts like the one shown on the right.

Tristan Slays the Beast *by Mac Harshberger*

EARLY VERSIONS

The tale of a Cornish knight and his doomed love for an Irish princess has been around for over two thousand years. But from 1190, European writers began to weave the story into the tale of King Arthur. In some versions, the love potion is only temporary, while in others it binds them for life. There is even one account where Iseult is sent to a leper colony by Mark as punishment for her deceit. Around 1210, Gottfried von Strasbourg wrote the classic account of the love story. A more famous version was written later by Thomas Malory.

Sir Mordred, by H.J. Ford

A QUEST FOR POWER

When Arthur leaves England to pursue Lancelot, he leaves Mordred in charge in his absence. But the deceitful knight exploits the position, and seizes the crown for himself. Mordred tells Arthur's subjects that the king is dead, and then abducts Guinevere in an attempt to force Arthur back to England for a final battle.

MORDRED THE MURDERER

Mordred is the knight responsible for exposing Lancelot and Guinevere's affair to Arthur. At the Battle of Camlann (*see pages 27-28*), he comes face to face with Arthur, who slays him. But as Mordred falls, the wicked knight drives a spear through the king's body, inflicting mortal wounds on him.

How Mordred was slain by Arthur, *by Arthur Rackham*

ARTHUR & MORGAUSE

Mordred is the product of an incestuous relationship between Arthur and his half-sister, Morgause, who seduces the king. When he becomes a man, Mordred joins the Round Table as one of Arthur's knights.

Morgause and Mordred in the film
The Mists of Avalon *(2001)*

FAMILY RIVALRIES

Left: Morgan Le Fay *by John Waterhouse*

Mordred and Morgan Le Fay are Arthur's main adversaries during his reign as king. Arthur's son Mordred first appears under the Cornish name Medraut in the *Annales Cambriae*, where it is said he dies at the Battle of Camlann where Arthur too perishes. However, it is not until Geoffrey of Monmouth's *Historia* that his role as the traitor is sealed. Morgan Le Fay is Arthur's half-sister, but she too turns against the king, using magical powers learnt under Merlin to plague him.

MAGICAL MORGAN

Morgan Le Fay first appears in Geoffrey of Monmouth's *Vita Merlini* as a woman with magical powers that enable her to change shape and even fly. In fact, her name actually means "the fairy". She is a pupil of Merlin and learns magic from him. In *Vita Merlini*, Morgan is the first of nine sisters who rule The Fortunate Isle (another name for the Isle of Avalon), and is presented as a healer as well as a shape-changer. In Malory's *Le Morte D'Arthur*, she actually appears on the barge that takes Arthur off to be healed at Avalon (*see p26-27*). She promises Arthur that she can heal the dreadful wounds he sustained at the Battle of Camlann if he stays with her.

SCHEMING SISTER

Morgan Le Fay is the daughter of Arthur's mother Igraine and her first husband, the Duke of Cornwall. Morgan Le Fay hates Arthur because his father Uther Pendragon slayed her father, and she comes up with several plots to bring about the king's downfall. In one, she hatches a plan with a knight called Accolon of Gaul to steal Excalibur and murder Arthur. The king eventually retrieves the sword, but the scabbard, which protects him on the battlefield, is lost. Another of Morgan's plots involves the kidnapping of Lancelot, but the knight escapes unharmed.

MORGAN & THE GREEN KNIGHT

Morgan Le Fay harbours a deep hatred of Arthur's queen Guinevere. Once a lady-in-waiting to the queen, Le Fay fell in love with Arthur's nephew, Guiomar, but Guinevere drove the couple apart. Morgan vows to get revenge, and in the poem *Sir Gawain and the Green Knight (see page 16)*, it is she who sends the Green Knight to Camelot to frighten the Queen.

Morgan Le Fay *by A.F.A. Sandys*

MAGIC & MONSTERS

A 19th-century illustration of a giant, a monster that appears in many Arthurian stories

During the age of Arthur, many writers tell us that the kingdom of Camelot and the lands beyond were infested with a number of frightening beasts. These ranged from ogres, witches and wizards to dragons and serpents. However, there were also a number of helpful magical beings. These ranged from gentle giants to animals that helped King Arthur and his followers in their battle against evil.

GIANTS & OGRES

Arthur's kingdom is filled with several giants. One of these monsters was called Rience. He wore a cloak made out of the beards of the kings he had killed, and sent a message to Arthur saying he would like to add the king's beard to his collection. In one story Rience is captured and brought to Arthur, while in another version Arthur kills him in combat. Not all giants were harmful, however. Gargantua was a giant whose father was created by Merlin from whale bones and blood from Lancelot. He served Arthur loyally, and fought the king's foes with a sixty-foot club.

A 19th-century illustration of one of the hags of Gloucester

HAGS OF GLOUCESTER

The hags of Gloucester were nine witches who had once trained the knight Perceval (*see page 25*) in armed combat. But they turned against the knight and beheaded his cousin, sending his head to Perceval on a platter. The witches were eventually destroyed by Arthur and Perceval.

DRAGONS & SERPENTS

In one version of the story of Tristan and Iseult (*see pages 18-19*), the King of Ireland offers his daughter Iseult's hand to anyone who will slay a fire-breathing dragon that has been plaguing his kingdom. The knight Tristan knows that water is fatal for fire dragons, and takes a flask to the monster's lair. There he douses the dragon with the water to quench his fire, and then battles him to the death.

Serpents also play a part in several Arthurian stories. In a French book called *Perceval le Gallois ou le conte du Graal* (AD 1300), the knight Perceval slays a monstrous serpent who has captured a maiden. When he slits the serpent's throat, he finds a key in its belly that he uses to free a knight unjustly imprisoned by a corrupt king.

CATH PALUG & THE QUESTING BEAST

One of the most terrible monsters Arthur faced was the Cath Palug, a monstrous cat with deadly claws. One tale says that Arthur killed it near Lake Bourget in France, but another says that it killed the King and conquered Britain. Another monster was the Questing Beast. It had the head of a snake, the body of a leopard, the hindquarters of a lion and the feet of a deer. It is said that forty hounds could be heard baying from inside its stomach.

An anonymous illustration of King Arthur and the Questing Beast

THE CHOUGH

The chough is a member of the crow family, and is the symbol of Cornwall. Cornish folklore tells a story about how it got its red beak and legs. The knight Murdoch hatches a plan to murder Guinevere, but he is overheard by Merlin's pet chough, a bird that can understand humans. It fights Murdoch and eventually kills him, just before King Arthur arrives. When Arthur finds the chough with blood on its beak and legs, he knights the bird, as a reward for its bravery. Ever since then, all choughs have a red beak and red legs.

LOYAL LIONS

Many Arthurian stories feature helpful lions. In Chrétien's *Yvain, or The Knight with the Lion*, the knight Yvain rescues a lion from a serpent. To thank him, the lion befriends Yvain, and helps him battle against many enemies during the knight's lifetime.

QUEST FOR THE HOLY GRAIL

hrétien De Troyes was the first writer to link a magical object called the *graal* with the story of King Arthur, in an unfinished poem called *Le Conte del Graal (1180)*. But it was not until the publication of three romances by Robert de Boron in 1200, that the Grail became a holy symbol. Boron describes a vessel used in the Last Supper that was also used by Joseph of Arimathea to catch Christ's blood spilt at his crucifixion. In Arthurian stories, the Holy Grail appears at the Round Table, and is pursued by several of King Arthur's knights.

THE MAGICAL GRAIL

Many writers suggest that the Holy Grail has special powers. In de Boron's story, the Grail is a magical chalice that can cure any ill, and even give those who drink from it eternal youth

The Damsel of the Sanct Grail, by Dante Gabriel Rossetti

A 15th-century French illustration showing the Grail appearing at the Round Table

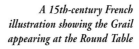

VISIONS AT THE ROUND TABLE

According to Thomas Malory, many years after it had arrived in Britain, the Holy Grail appeared to the knights seated around the Round Table. Malory says it was "covered in a rich silk, and filled the room with fragrance, as if all the spices of the earth had been scattered there." As the Grail moves around the table, it grants to each knight whatever they desire to eat. When they have all dined, the cup disappears. The knights swear an oath to find the Grail, and the following morning they ride out from Camelot in search of it.

GODLY GALAHAD

The knight Galahad first appears in the 13th-century *Vulgate Cycle* stories (*see page 32*), and is seen as the perfect knight, combining chivalry, honour, love and loyalty. Galahad is the son of Lancelot and Elaine of Corbenic. Elaine's father, King Pelles, encourages his daughter to trick Lancelot into sleeping with her (*see page 14*), aided by the sorceror Brusen. This is because Lancelot was thought to be a blood-descendant of Christ. Pelles believed that the birth of such a boy would heal his brother, the Maimed King (*see page 25*), and bring peace and prosperity back to the kingdom. Galahad searches for the Grail with the knights Perceval and Bors, but because of his virtue, Galahad is the only one of Arthur's knights to discover the Grail's true meaning.

Sir Galahad by G.F. Watts

PERCEVAL & BORS

Galahad is part of a trio of knights of unblemished virtue known as the peerless knights. The others are Perceval and Bors. Galahad meets Perceval in a forest, where the knight mistakes him for an enemy, and nearly kills him. But Galahad survives, and the two become devoted friends.

The third peerless knight, Bors, is renowned for his courage, and spends his whole life trying to uphold the Code of Chivalry (*see page 12*). The vision of the Holy Grail is also experienced by Perceval's sister, the nun Dindrane. She arms Galahad with the Sword of David, and the pair set off on their quest, together with Perceval and Bors.

How Sir Galahad, Sir Bors and Sir Percival Were Fed with the Sanc Grael by Dante Gabriel Rossetti

Harrison Ford and Sean Connery in the film **Indiana Jones and the Last Crusade**

THE FISHER KING & THE GRAIL CASTLE

Stories tell us that when the Holy Grail arrived in Britain, it needed to be guarded day and night. This task fell to a man called the Fisher King. His name was Bran, and he lived in a castle in Wales. Bran bore battle wounds that would not heal, and these scars resulted in the nickname *The Maimed King*. He is eventually healed by Galahad when the knight reached the Fisher King's castle, and he tells Galahad the true meaning of the Grail. Films such as *Indiana Jones and the Last Crusade* (1993) tell this gripping story, with Sean Connery as the Maimed King being healed by the Grail Knight in the form of Harrison Ford.

Tailpiece of Arthur and his knights, from a medieval account of the search for the Holy Grail.

THE END OF THE TRAIL

After the Maimed King is healed, Malory tell us that the three knights and Dindrane follow the Grail to Sarras, mythical land of the Saracens. There, Galahad drinks from the cup, and experiences an incredible vision. His spirit ascends to Heaven with the chalice. Perceval remains in the East as a hermit, while Bors returns to Camelot.

CHANGING GRAIL KNIGHTS

In the early Grail stories, the knight Perceval was the only knight to seek the Grail. In Chrétien's Le Conte del Graal (see page 22), it is Perceval who finds the Grail Castle, but fails in his quest to understand the mysteries of the Holy Grail. Later writers have Perceval succeeding in his mission, but when Lancelot became more and more important in Arthurian romance, his son Galahad took over the role of Grail knight. Galahad was immortalised in that role in Malory's Le Morte D'Arthur.

A medieval illustration showing Mordred's guards outside Guinevere's chamber

CAMELOT CAPTURED

Together with his brother, the knight Agravaine, Mordred (*see page 22*) plots to reveal Lancelot and Guinevere's affair. When they catch Lancelot in the Queen's chamber, King Arthur sentences Guinevere to death, but Lancelot rescues her and escapes to France. Gawain convinces the King that they should pursue the pair, and when they meet, Gawain challenges Lancelot to a duel. During a fight, Gawian suffers serious wounds that will eventually kill him. While Arthur and Gawain are away, Mordred seizes his chance to claim the throne, aided and supported by many young knights who knew little of the struggle Arthur put into building up Camelot.

THE DOWNFALL OF ARTHUR

By the time the Grail Quest had finished, the lustre of Arthur's Camelot had started to fade. Many knights had left the Round Table, and others were becoming disenchanted with Arthur's kingdom. Lancelot was often away, and Perceval was living as a hermit in the Holy Land. When Lancelot's affair was exposed by Mordred, it brought about a chain of events that would end in bloodshed and the collapse of Camelot.

BATTLE OF CAMLANN

According to Geoffrey of Monmouth, the Battle of Camlann took place around 539 AD. When Arthur returns to Britain to reclaim his kingdom, his army mass up against Mordred's men. The two armies then come face to face at Camlann. Swords are drawn, and a bloody battle begins. According to Malory, at the end of hostilities only Arthur, Bedivere and Mordred survive. When Mordred charges at Arthur, the king strikes him with a fatal blow, but as he dies Mordred strikes Arthur on the head with a heavy sword. Because Arthur no longer has Excalibur's scabbard to protect him on the battlefield, the king suffers terrible injuries.

Scene from the Battle of Camlann in the film Excalibur (1981)

THE END OF ARTHUR

After the fight at Camlann, Arthur is carried from the battlefield by the knights Sir Bedivere and Sir Lucan. Arthur asks Sir Bedivere to throw his sword Excalibur back into the lake from which it came, but for a while the knight finds himself unable to return the sword. Eventually he flings it into the water, where a woman emerges, draped all in white, to reclaim the blade. A ghostly ship then approaches the shore carrying three queens, including the Lady of the Lake and Morgan le Fay. Arthur is then taken to Avalon, where the queens attend to his dreadful wounds. Neither Malory nor Geoffrey of Monmouth tell us if Arthur died there, so the story is left open.

A painting by Sir Joseph Paton showing Arthur in his death barge on the way to Avalon

DEAD OR ALIVE?

According to one story, many years later Sir Bedivere visits a monastery in Glastonbury, where he finds a gravestone with a Latin inscription that reads *"Here lies Arthur, the Once and Future King."* This line was picked up by later romantic writers to weave a myth about Arthur's immortality. These accounts suggest that the king will return when the country needs his leadership most.

King Arthur's statue in Royal Chapel at Innsbruck in Austria.

Medieval illustration showing the Wild Hunt

THE FAERIE REALM

According to writers such as Malory, the Isle of Avalon was the home of the Faerie Realm. King Arthur was taken there after being mortally wounded and attended by three faerie queens. Avalon was probably based on a Celtic otherworld called Tir na n-Oc or Land of Youth. This world crops up in several Arthurian poems.

ARTHUR THE GHOST

Some stories say that Arthur was not killed at Camlann, but instead he lay sleeping in an underground cavern, waiting for the right time to return and reign again. Another account depicts Arthur as the leader of the Wild Hunt, a crowd of ghosts who go riding at midday or on nights when there is a full moon. The location of the hunt varies, but in England people claim to have seen it in Devon and Somerset.

Tintagel in Cornwall

Peaceful Camlan in Wales

TINTAGEL

The fictional Arthur that we have come to know best was born at Tintagel Castle in North Cornwall. Today the village is overrun in the summer season with tourists who have come to visit the birthplace of a king. Unfortunately, however, the castle that stands at Tintagel in Cornwall cannot possibly be the birthplace of King Arthur, because it only dates from the 12th century. But in the 1930s archaeologists discovered thousands of pieces of Mediterranean pottery on the site. They dated from between 400-600 AD, and showed that Tintagel had been a place of great importance during Arthur's reign.

CAMLANN

Camlann was the site of Arthur's final battle. Although Malory identified the battlefield with Salisbury Plain, no evidence has been found to prove this theory. Other candidates include Slaughter Bridge on the River Camel in Cornwall, and a place called Camlan in Wales. The latter is the only place in Britain ever to have had the name Camlan. It is also mentioned by both Geoffrey of Monmouth and the Welsh Annales.

AVALON *&* GLASTONBURY

The town of Glastonbury in Somerset has been said to be the site of Avalon, the final resting place of King Arthur. Geoffrey of Monmouth tells us that Arthur was nursed there after the battle of Camlann. Then in 1190 AD, monks rebuilding the old abbey in Glastonbury claimed to have uncovered the bones of a tall man in a grave marked with a lead cross bearing a Latin phrase which means *Here lies the renowned King Arthur in the isle of Avalon with his second wife Guinevere.* However, nothing exists there today, and the inscription has been condemned by language experts as a fraud.

Glastonbury Abbey in Somerset

KING ARTHUR'S WORLD

Today many places in Britain and Europe claim an association with Arthur. From Tintagel on the south coast of Cornwall to Brittany and beyond, Arthur's world has grown considerably since the first writings of Gildas. Through the use of archaeological methods such as carbon dating and dendrochronology (*see page 9*) historians have been able to eliminate certain sites to try to locate where exactly the legendary king may have lived.

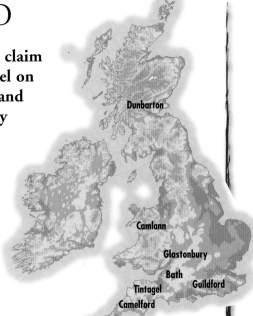

Dunbarton
Camlann
Glastonbury
Bath
Tintagel
Guildford
Camelford

SHALOTT/ASTALOT

Shalott was the home of Elaine of Astalot, whose heart was broken by the knight Lancelot. Malory says it was in Guildford in Surrey, but its true location was more likely to have been Dunbarton in Scotland, which was called Alclut in ancient times.

A lonely beach in Dunbarton

BATH & BADON HILL

The Battle of Badon (*see page 7*) was the scene of Arthur's most famous victory, where he repelled the Saxon mercenaries and brought peace to his kingdom. Historians have for a long time tried to locate the site of the battle. Geoffrey of Monmouth tells us that it was Bath. Similarly, Nennius says that Badon was a place "with a hot lake, where the baths of Badon are," possibly a reference to the Roman Baths in the city. Bath is also called Badanceaster, the City of Badan. Evidence has also been found that says Bath was once called Bathon.

The impressive Roman baths in the city of Bath

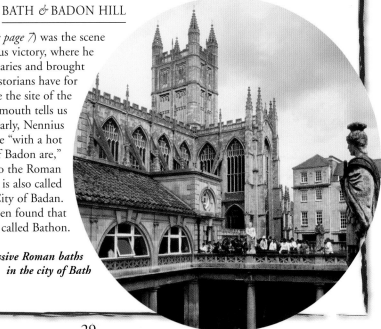

29

KING ARTHUR TODAY

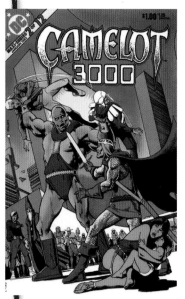

Cover of Camelot 3000

Although if Arthur ever lived, he would have died over a thousand years ago, his legend endures in fiction, film and popular culture. Arthur has even been updated for the new millennium. He appears in comic books and video games, and on thousands of websites across the world.

ARTHURIAN FICTION

During the early 20th century, Arthur fell out of fashion. The stark and brutal realities of World War I sat uncomfortably with tales of chivalry and gallantry. Then in the 1920s, poets such as T.S Eliot started writing about Arthur again. Today Arthurian fiction ranges from novels by Rosemary Sutcliff and plays by John Arden to science-fiction epics. There are even comic strips which pitch the king into the future, where he takes up the eternal battle of good against evil. In *Camelot 3000*, King Arthur is brought back to life in AD 3000 to save the world from an alien invasion.

The stage show King Arthur, performed in Las Vegas

Scene from Monty Python and the Holy Grail

ARTHUR & TOURISM

Visitors to Britain and other parts of Europe will be struck by how many locations today claim to be the home of the great King. From Brittany in France to Tintagel in Cornwall and Glastonbury in Somerset, a flourishing tourist trade has built up around the legend of King Arthur. There is an annual hippy pilgrimage to Glastonbury while even in the United States, companies have started offering Arthurian holidays.

T.H.WHITE

The Cambridge graduate T.H. White produced the most important modern book on Arthur. His novel The Once and Future King (1958) retells the Arthurian legend, filling in gaps including Arthur's education by Merlin. The book also gives the knights of the Round Table vibrant personalities. Rather than attempting to put Arthur in an historical context, White jumps from late medieval chivalry to early 20th-century themes. He also makes political comments in the book. Arthur's motto of "Might for right" contrasts with the dictatorships that existed in parts of Europe when the book was published.

LAUGHING WITH ARTHUR

In 1975, the British comedy team behind the *Monty Python* series launched a film called *Monty Python and the Holy Grail*. An irreverent look at the legend, it shows a Camelot full of slapstick and satire, but the film also displays a deep knowledge of the historical Arthur and of the medieval period in general.

A scene from the film Excalibur *(1981)*

MOVIE KING

Arthur made one of his earliest appearances on the screen back in 1921, in the silent movie *A Connecticut Yankee in King Arthur's Court*. In the 1940s and 1950s, a series of swashbuckling adventures featured the king in more heroic guise. Then in 1967, the film *Camelot* was launched, starring Richard Harris and Vanessa Redgrave. The film concentrates on the love triangle between Arthur, Guinevere and Lancelot.

More recent films have included the Disney cartoon *The Sword in the Stone* (1963), *Excalibur* (1981), and *First Knight* (1995), starring Julia Ormond, Richard Gere and Sean Connery.

ARTHUR ON THE INTERNET

King Arthur has even been embraced by a cyber audience. Today Arthur enthusiasts can log on to the Web to take part in role-playing Arthurian adventures, and join newsgroups dedicated to King Arthur. Academics can also carry out serious research making use of the increasing number of medieval manuscripts posted onto the World Wide Web.

A selection of Arthurian websites

DID YOU KNOW?

There are several different stories about Arthur's knights, and their quest for the Holy Grail.

CHRÉTIEN DE TROYES' CONTE DEL GRAAL

The *Conte del Graal* was the first Grail story. In this tale, a young boy called Perceval, raised in the woods by his mother, sees a group of knights in gleaming armour, and vows to become one himself when he grows up. Eventually Perceval joins Arthur's court and sets off on a quest for the Holy Grail. When he finds the Grail Castle, the Grail appears in front of him. However, Perceval fails to ask what the Grail is and who it should serve, questions that would have healed the Fisher King. The next day he awakes to find himself in the wilderness.

DIDOT-PERCEVAL

This prose piece was written by an anonymous French poet between 1200-1230. In this poem Perceval sits in the forbidden thirteenth chair at the Round Table, the Siege Perilous (*see page 12*), plunging Britain into darkness. This darkness will only end when the Grail is found. Eventually Perceval finds the Grail, and brings light back to Arthur's kingdom.

PARZIVAL

Parzival was written around 1210 by the German writer Wolfram von Eschenbach. In this story, Parzival joins the Round Table, and experiences a vision of the Holy Grail. Parzival fails in his first quest to find the cup, but he later returns to complete his mission, healing the Fisher King.

ROBERT DE BORON

The Frenchman Robert de Boron was responsible for making the Grail the cup of Christ. In the first of three unnamed stories written around the turn of the 13th century, he follows the Grail's journey from the Christ's Crucifixion to the arrival of Joseph of Arimathea (guardian of Christ's body after his death) in the West with the Grail and the Bleeding Lance. On the way, a mass is held at a round table, and Joseph's brother-in-law, Bron is appointed the guardian of the Grail (the Fisher King). Bron and his sons travel to the Vales of Avalon, where they await the arrival of the "third man" from Arthur's Round Table, to become the ultimate keeper of the Grail.

PERLESVAUS

This 13th-century French story mixes the story of Perceval and the Holy Grail with the legend of Arthur and Camelot. In *Perlesvaus*, Gauvain and Lancelot fail in their quests for the Grail, but Perceval succeeds, avenging his mother, freeing the Grail castle from an evil figure called the King of Castle Mortal, and restoring peace and prosperity to Arthur's kingdom.

VULGATE CYCLE

Written between 1215-1235, the *Vulgate Cycle* introduces Sir Galahad as the new Grail knight. Here, he is believed to be a blood descendant of Christ, and the only knight capable of healing the Maimed King (Fisher King). Along with Perceval and Bors, Galahad finds the Grail, but only Galahad discovers its true meaning.

ACKNOWLEDGEMENTS

We would also like to thank: Graham Rich and Elizabeth Wiggans for their assistance and David Hobbs for his map of the world. Picture research by Image Select. Printed in China. Copyright © 2005 ticktock Media Ltd.

No part of this publication may be reproduced, stored in a retrieval system, or transmitted in any form or by any means, electronic, mechanical, photocopying, recording or otherwise, without prior written permission of the copyright owner.

A CIP Catalogue for this book is available from the British Library. ISBN 1 86007 414 6

Alamy: 4t, 5b, 11b, 14b, 29b, 29cl, 30cr. Album Online: IBC, 7r, 8c, 10t, 13b, 20b, 25c, 26b, 31t. Bridgeman Art Library: 2t, 6c, 15c, 19l, 20cl. Collections Photo Library: 16-17b. Corbis: 2b, 3b, 5cr, 6l & OFC, 9br, 12t, 27tr, 28b, 30c. Fortean Picture Library: 3tr, 7t, 12b, 13t, 23t, 24c, 25b.

Every effort has been made to trace the copyright holders and we apologise in advance for any unintentional omissions. We would be pleased to insert the appropriate acknowledgement in any subsequent edition of this publication.

snapping-turtle guide